D0385375

This edition published by Parragon in 2012
Parragon
Queen Street House
4 Queen Street
Bath BA1 1HE, UK
www.parragon.com



ISBN 978-1-4454-8668-0

Printed in China

Disney · PIXAR

# BRAVE

## MAGICAL STORY

Adapted by Barbara Bazaldua

Illustrated by Studio Iboix and Maria Elena Naggi
and the Disney Storybook Artists

Bath • New York • Singapore • Hong Kong • Cologne • Delhi
Melbourne • Amsterdam • Johannesburg • Auckland • Shenzhen

Merida, the Princess of DunBroch, loved archery. She loved her horse, Angus. And she loved to roam the Scottish Highlands where she lived with her mother, father and three younger brothers.

But Merida did not love it when her parents, King Fergus and Queen Elinor, said she should marry a son from a neighbouring clan.

"I'm not ready to marry!"
Merida shouted.

The clans gathered and the lords presented their eldest sons to Merida. Then the queen announced that Merida would choose a competition for the sons.

"I choose archery!"
Merida declared.

The crowd watched as the three sons competed. When they were done, Merida stepped onto the field.

"I'll be shooting for my own hand!" she announced. Three times her arrows hit their marks. She was the winner!

Elinor dragged Merida inside. Merida did not understand that this could lead to war among the clans!

"I'll never be like you!" Merida slashed the family tapestry!

Sobbing, Merida rode Angus deep into the forest until they came upon a majestic ring of stones. Glowing wisps beckoned her to follow them to a witch's cottage.

Long ago, the Witch had helped a prince gain great strength. Merida wanted help in changing her mum's mind. The Witch reluctantly agreed and created a magic cake.

Eagerly, Merida returned home. Her father was stalling the suitors by telling of Mor'du, a fierce bear who had taken his leg. She also found her mother... **and gave her the cake.**

But instead of changing Elinor's mind about the marriage, the cake changed her into a bear! Merida helped Elinor-Bear sneak past Fergus and the clans to escape into the forest.

They couldn't find the Witch, but they found a riddle: "Fate be changed, look inside, mend the bond torn by pride." The next morning, Merida taught a hungry Elinor-Bear to fish. They had fun – but Elinor was starting to act like a real bear.

Desperate, Merida explored the ruins of an ancient castle with a picture of its four princes. There were deep, angry claw marks all around – marks from the Witch's prince! With his great strength, he had become a bear – **Mor'du**! And he had ruined the kingdom with his greed.

Elinor-Bear and Merida raced home. Merida needed the tapestry to "mend the bond torn by pride." But first she faced the clans. With her mother's help, she proposed that she and her suitors be free to follow their hearts. Cheers rang out!

Then Fergus found Merida with Elinor-Bear. Not recognizing his wife, the king locked Merida in the Tapestry Room to keep her safe. Then he and the other men chased Elinor like a wild bear!

Merida saw three bear cubs in the hall. Her brothers had eaten the remaining spell cake.

"Get the key!" she told them. The cubs chased the housekeeper, snatched the key and set Merida free!

With the cubs by her side, Merida stitched the tapestry as they raced to save Elinor-Bear.

But Fergus and the clans had already trapped Elinor-Bear in the Ring of Stones.

"I'll not let you kill my mother!" Merida told her father.

Suddenly, Mor'du lunged at Merida from the shadows. With a roar, Elinor-Bear broke free and charged. After a terrifying battle, Elinor-Bear defeated Mor'du once and for all.

Merida threw the tapestry over her mother the bear. But nothing happened. "I want you back, Mum. I love you!" Merida sobbed.

And finally, with dawn's new light, the spell broke. And mother and daughter knew that the bond between them was mended at last.